The Birdman

WILLEMIEN MIN

E. P. DUTTON · NEW YORK

I was on the balcony the day the Birdman came. I heard sweet music in the street below, coming from the strange-looking man playing an accordion. At least I think he was a man. He wore a long coat, but he had a face like a bird's.

Other children must have heard the music too, for soon he was leading a procession. I ran outside to join them. All of us brought our toy birds. I held mine up high.

But then something strange happened. All by them-
selves the wings on my bird started to move in time
to the music. He began to grow, and soon was big
enough to pull me off the ground. It was as if he were
alive! I held on tightly as he rose higher and higher.
We were flying!

All the children were flying.
It was like a fairy tale.

But then my arms began to get tired, and I didn't think I could hold on for much longer. My bird was flying right into the wind. I knew I had to climb onto his back or I would fall. It was difficult, but I did it.

Riding there, I could see far away in the distance. Ahead the sky was dull and gray and full of clouds. But we flew on, right into the dark. A fierce wind blew all around us.

Suddenly I heard a crack. Oh no!

My sea gull's stick broke. His wing hung down and could no longer move. I thought we were going to fall, but the birds came to our rescue. Daniel's took me on his back. The others caught my bird's strings in their sturdy beaks and brought him safely through the storm.

As if by magic, the sky cleared.
Beneath us was an island.

Birds were everywhere. Some had seen us coming and flew to meet us. Others came out of little houses and flapped their wings in greeting. It looked like a good place to rest after our long journey.

We had a wonderful party there, with cakes and lemonade for everyone. My bird's wing was fixed so he could fly again. One of the birds told me this was a place where toy birds could live when children no longer wanted to play with them. The Birdman brought them to life with his music and led them here—to Bird Island. Sometimes before that, toy birds were allowed to visit. They brought children with them, but they always took the children back.

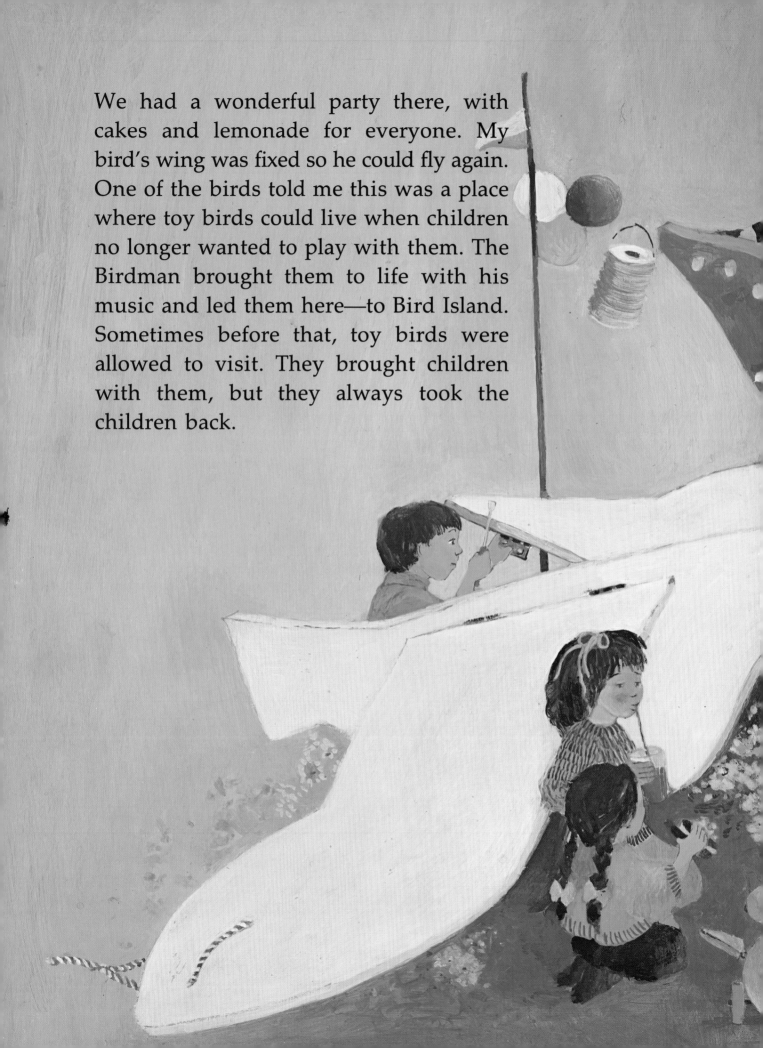

The Birdman! We had forgotten all about him. But then we heard his music, and there he was. All too soon it was time to say good-bye to the other birds and go home.

Now my bird seems like a toy again. He is small, and his wings move only when I pull the strings. When I see him, I think about Bird Island. Then I pick him up and play with him.